To Be a Cowboy

by
Bonnie Highsmith Taylor

Perfection Learning®

Cover Illustration: Kay McCabe
Inside Illustration: Kay McCabe

About the Author
Bonnie Highsmith Taylor is a native Oregonian. She loves camping in the Oregon mountains and watching birds and other wildlife. Writing is Ms. Taylor's first love. But she also enjoys going to plays and concerts, collecting antique dolls, and listening to good music.

Perfection Learning® Corporation,
1000 North Second Avenue,
P.O. Box 500, Logan, Iowa 51546-1099.
Phone: 1-800-831-4190 • Fax: 1-712-644-2392

Paperback ISBN 0-7891-2901-9
Cover Craft® ISBN 0-7807-8155-4

Contents

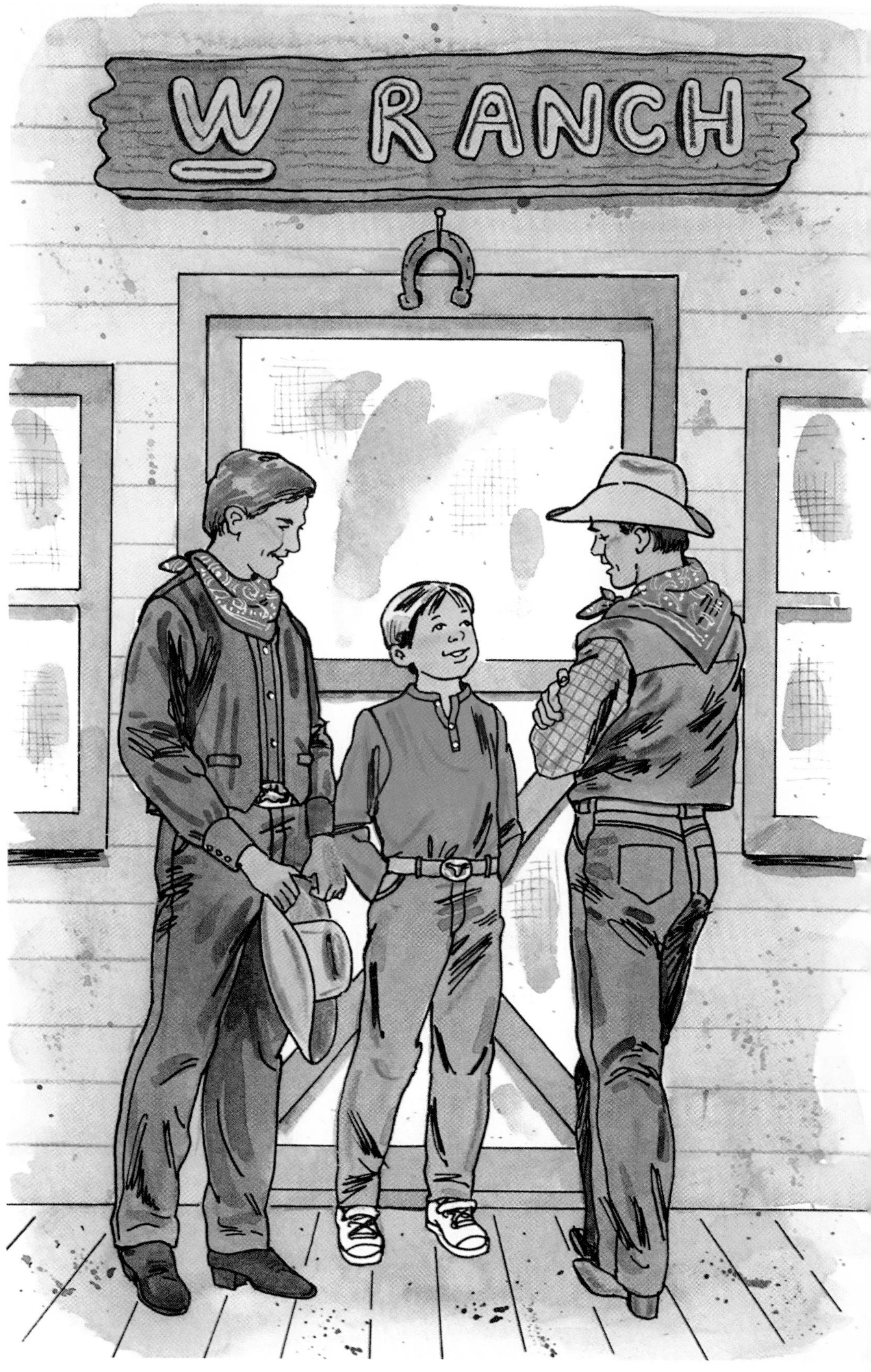
W RANCH

Chapter 1

Bar W Ranch

Eddie wanted to be a cowboy.

His Uncle Hank was a cowboy. Uncle Charlie was one too.

They worked on the Bar W Ranch. They slept in the bunkhouse. When Eddie visited, he had his own bunk. It was under Uncle Charlie's. Uncle Hank's bunk was on the same wall.

A big iron stove stood in the middle of the room. It burned wood.

Eddie thought the bunkhouse was great. Nobody cared if it was messy. Some of the cowboys didn't even wipe their feet.

One cowboy was named Slim. He told Eddie, "You can hang your clothes on the wall pegs." Then he grinned. "Or you can hang them on the floor. Like I do."

Eddie laughed. He decided he would use the wall pegs.

Eddie liked all the men. Some of them had nicknames like Slim. Tex was from Texas. Sandy had red hair and freckles. Shorty, of course, was short.

Bud and Tim were brothers. They played

guitars and sang. Eddie thought they were very good.

Old Ben was the oldest man on the ranch. Eddie liked him best. Except for his uncles.

Ben told a lot of stories about the old days. He told about when he was a young cowboy. And when he went on long trail drives.

Old Ben played a banjo. He sang too. He sang the old cowboy songs. He was teaching them to Eddie.

Once Old Ben sang a song called "Git Along, Little Dogies."

"You mean 'doggies,' don't you?" asked Eddie.

"No, Eddie," Ben replied. "A *dogie* is a calf that has no mother. It's an orphan."

The ranch house was huge. It had a porch on two sides. It was three stories high.

Old Ben said, "Where that house stands, there was once a one-room log cabin. The owner's great-grandfather built it. About 100 years ago.

"The first bunkhouse was a tent," he said. "And so was the first cook shack."

"Wow!" exclaimed Eddie.

The cook shack now was as big as the bunkhouse.

Sugar Sam was the cook. He slept in a corner of the cook shack on a cot.

The cowboys called him Sugar Sam because he put so much sugar in his coffee.

Eddie liked eating in the cook shack. He liked Sam's biscuits and stew. But most of all, he liked Sam's flapjacks and ham.

There were two big barns on the ranch. There were lots of other buildings. One was a blacksmith shop. Others were storage sheds.

Old Ben told Eddie, "I started herding cows long ago. When I was 15 years old."

"He's forgotten more than we'll ever know," said Uncle Charlie.

"That's right," Uncle Hank agreed. "He was a good cowboy."

Some of the other cowboys said, "He taught us everything we know."

"I don't ride much anymore," said Ben. "I'm the blacksmith. I shoe the horses. I take care of the tack. Keep it in good shape. And I do odd jobs around the ranch."

"What's 'tack'?" asked Eddie.

"I'll show you" said Ben. "Follow me."

Chapter 2

Tack

Eddie followed Ben to a shed. Inside were lots of saddles. Leather things hung on the wall.

"This is the tack room," said Old Ben. "Tack is *riding gear.*"

"It smells good," Eddie said.

Old Ben smiled. "Some folks don't think so. Me, I've always liked the smell of leather."

The saddles rested on a long, round pole.

"These are Western saddles," Ben said. "This thing sticking up here is called a *saddle horn.*"

"A horn!" exclaimed Eddie.

Ben laughed. "Not the kind of horn that honks," he said. "The saddle horn is very important to a cowboy. It's where he hangs his rope. He also holds onto it to mount his horse."

Ben lifted Eddie onto a saddle. Eddie ran his hands over the leather. He grabbed the horn. He liked the way it felt. He tried to reach the stirrups. They were too long.

"Don't worry," said Ben. "They can be made shorter. Your uncles will rig up a saddle for you."

"Cool!" said Eddie.

"You'll be riding in no time. To be a cowboy, you must be a good rider."

Eddie got off the saddle. He pointed to some straps on the lower part of the saddle.

"What are those?" he asked.

Ben said, "Those are *cinches.* They go under the horse's belly. They are pulled tight to hold the saddle in place."

Ben took one of the leather things off the wall.

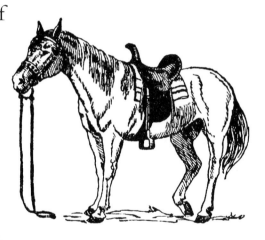

"This is a *bridle,*" he said. "It fits over the horse's head. This metal piece is a *bit.* It goes in the horse's mouth."

"Doesn't it hurt? asked Eddie.

"Not if it's used right," said Ben. "These straps that come from both sides of the bit are *reins.*"

"I know what they're for," said Eddie. "To steer the horse."

Old Ben smiled. "You could say that. A good cowboy can guide his horse with a flick of the reins on its neck. Or with a gentle tug left or right."

Ben went on. "The very first cowboys rode bareback. So did Indians. The first saddle was just a blanket. It was held in place with rawhide strips."

"But how did the riders steer their horses?" Eddie asked.

"By pressing their knees against the horse's body. Or with a pat on its neck." Ben answered.

Eddie asked, "Can you ride a horse bareback?"

"I'd probably break my neck if I tried now," said the old cowboy. "I did when I was no bigger than you. But it was because I didn't have a saddle."

Old Ben sat down on a wooden bench. "I used to ride bareback in rodeos," he went on. "And I was pretty good. Even if I do say so myself."

"Really?" exclaimed Eddie.

Ben laughed. "I wasn't always this old, young fella."

"I sure wish I could be a cowboy," said Eddie.

"You will be," said Ben. "On your next visit, your uncles will have a horse ready. And you'll have your first riding lesson."

Chapter 3

Horses

The horse's name was Smoky. Uncle Charlie helped Eddie into the saddle.

"Here are the reins," said Uncle Hank. "Don't yank on them. Pull very gently to turn."

Eddie liked sitting in the saddle. He felt so grown-up.

Uncle Hank mounted his horse, Rex. He rode on the right side of Eddie.

Uncle Charlie mounted his horse, Duke. He rode on Eddie's left.

They rode slowly away from the ranch.

Uncle Hank said, "You need to understand horses to be a cowboy."

"That's right," agreed Uncle Charlie. "And nothing works better on a horse than kindness."

"A cowboy and his horse can almost read each other's minds," said Uncle Hank. "Rex here is a *cutting horse*. A good cutting horse is worth a lot."

"What does 'cutting' mean?" asked Eddie.

"It means to cut or separate a cow from the herd," replied his uncle. "A cutting horse is smart. Sometimes a rider doesn't even need to use the reins. The horse does the work. And the thinking."

Eddie looked at Rex. He didn't look special. He was just a plain brown horse.

Eddie thought Duke was pretty.

Uncle Charlie said he was a strawberry roan. "But don't judge a horse by its color," he said. "Duke is a *roper.* He holds the reins tight when I rope a steer. He knows just how hard to pull back. A good roping horse is important."

"What is Smoky?" Eddie asked.

"A good herding horse," said Uncle Charlie. "And a brush horse."

"The best I ever saw," Uncle Hank added.

"Cows that leave the herd are called *outlaws*," said Uncle Charlie. "They hide in

thick brush. Some horses won't go in the brush. The ones that will are called *brush horses.*"

Eddie felt proud to be riding a special horse.

Uncle Hank said, "A night horse is special too. Not all horses work well in the dark."

After a while, they headed back to the ranch.

Uncle Charlie said, "First we'll water the horses. Then we'll feed them."

"They shouldn't drink too much water after eating. Their stomachs might swell."

Eddie helped comb Smoky with a currycomb. Smoky loved it.

When Eddie got home, he went to the library. He checked out books about horses. He learned a lot of things.

A *foal* is a newborn horse. It can be a male or a female. A *colt* is a young male horse. A *filly* is a young female horse. A *dam* is the mother of a foal. A *sire* is the father of a foal.

Some things Eddie learned surprised him.

"The first horses were brought from Spain," he told his mother and father. "Almost 500 years ago!

"The biggest horse is a Belgian," Eddie said. "It can

weigh 2,400 pounds. The smallest horse is a Shetland Pony. Some are only 300 pounds.

"Listen to this," he said. "The earliest kind of horse was only 10 to 20 inches high. It lived 65 million years ago!"

Eddie went back to visit the ranch.

The cowboys were amazed at the things he had learned.

"Pretty smart," said Tex. "For a tenderfoot."

Chapter 4

Roping and Branding

Soon it was time to learn roping.

"You need to be a good roper," said Slim. "To be a good cowboy."

"A cowboy can't work without a rope," said Tex.

All the men came to watch. Even Sugar Sam, the cook.

"A cowboy who can't rope," said Sam, "isn't worth his salt."

"Or his sugar," said Old Ben.

The other cowboys laughed.

"We'll start with that fence post." said Uncle Hank. "I'll make a lasso."

Uncle Hank showed Eddie how to hold a rope. He showed Eddie how to whirl the looped end. Around and around. Over his head.

Uncle Hank threw the rope. It fell around the fence post.

"Bull's-eye!" yelled the men.

"That looks easy," said Eddie. But the next thing he knew, the rope was wrapped around his own neck.

The cowboys all laughed. Eddie laughed too.

"I guess it's not as easy as it looks," he said.

"Don't feel bad," said Uncle Charlie. "We've all done the same thing."

"That's right," Old Ben agreed. "It takes a lot of practice."

Eddie learned a lot about roping. Just by watching and listening to the cowboys. He learned there were many kinds of loops. Some loops were for roping a steer by the horns. Some for roping a leg.

Eddie's head was spinning. He wondered how he would learn everything he needed to know to be a cowboy.

"You have to rope a calf to brand it," Sandy explained.

Eddie didn't like the idea of branding. Burning cows with hot irons sounded mean.

"It must hurt really bad," he said.

"I'm sure it does," said Uncle Charlie. "That's why it should be done fast."

"Cows need to be branded. That way ranchers can prove they own them," said Tim.

Old Ben said, "Brands are registered. A brand used by one rancher can't be used by another."

"There are hundreds of brands," said Tex. "Maybe thousands."

"Rustlers used to change brands," said Sugar Sam. "For example, a *C* could be changed to an *O.*"

"A *V* could be changed to a *W,*" added Old Ben. "There are many ways to change brands."

Eddie had seen the ranch cattle brand. It was a straight line. With a *W* over it. The line meant bar. Bar W.

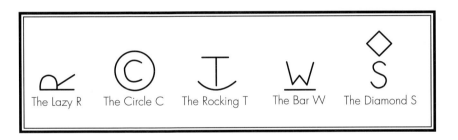

The Lazy R   The Circle C   The Rocking T   The Bar W   The Diamond S

The cowboys explained some of the brands. If a letter leaned to one side, it meant lazy. A leaning *R* would be Lazy R.

A letter *C* inside a circle was Circle C. A curved line meant rocking. A *T* over a curved line was a Rocking T. A diamond over an *S* would be Diamond S.

After supper, Bud and Tim played their guitars. They sang songs. Eddie sang along too.

Old Ben played the banjo. He taught Eddie some more old songs. Eddie liked "Ragtime Cowboy Joe."

"I want to be a cowboy. So should I learn to play a guitar?" asked Eddie. "Or a banjo?"

"Good idea," said Old Ben. "You have a fine voice."

Ben said, "Old-time cowboys played harmonicas. Or Jew's harps. Some took guitars and banjos on drives. But they took up a lot of room."

Old Ben was singing "Riding Old Paint."

Eddie began to get sleepy. Uncle Charlie led him into the bunkhouse. He tucked Eddie into bed. It had been a long day.

Chapter 5

Cowboy Duds

Eddie had new jeans and a new black western shirt. A red bandanna was tied around his neck. He wore a leather vest, new high-heeled boots, and a cowboy hat.

"Look at the dude!" laughed Tex.

"He won't be a dude long," said Ben. "He'll break in those duds. In no time."

Sandy said, "Wonder if that hat will fit me."

He put the hat on his head. He pranced around the bunkhouse.

"How about those boots?" said Slim. "Pretty nice."

"They feel a little tight," said Eddie. "They're hard to walk in."

"Cowboys don't walk," laughed Uncle Charlie. "They ride."

"Boots should be snug," said Old Ben. "They should fit like gloves."

"They pinch my toes," said Eddie.

"They'll stretch some," Uncle Hank said.

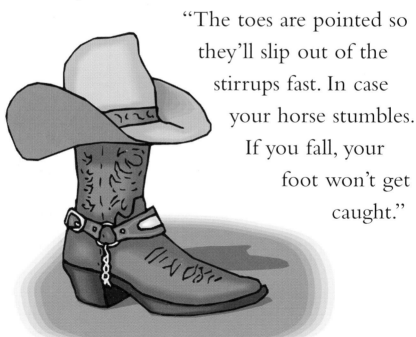

"The toes are pointed so they'll slip out of the stirrups fast. In case your horse stumbles. If you fall, your foot won't get caught."

"It feels funny walking in high heels," Eddie said.

"Heels are high for a reason," said Bud. "They hold the stirrup firmly."

"You'll get used to them," Old Ben said. "Some old-time cowboys soaked their boots in water. They wore them until the boots dried. It made them more snug."

"The high tops keep out rocks and other things," said Tim. "And they protect you from snakebites."

"The fancy stitching makes the leather stiff," explained Uncle Hank. "That keeps the boots from wrinkling. And becoming too sloppy."

"That's a good pair of boots," one cowboy said. "A good hat too."

"A cowboy's hat is important," said Uncle Charlie. "It keeps off the sun. It keeps the rain off your neck. In cold weather, you can pull the brim down over your ears."

"I've even watered me and my horse from my hat," said Ben. "And used it to beat out a grass fire."

"And to fan a campfire to life," added Sugar Sam.

"Wow!" Eddie exclaimed. "Everything a cowboy wears is good for something."

"There's one more thing you need," said Old Ben.

"What?" asked Eddie.

"A pair of spurs." Ben pulled a wooden box from under his bunk. "I have an extra pair."

He put them on Eddie's boots. "I'll work on them tomorrow," he said. "Make them fit better."

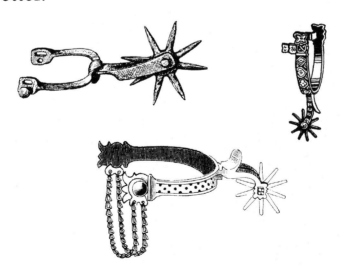

Eddie walked around and around. He liked the way the spurs jingled.

"When you're a working cowboy, you'll need chaps," said Uncle Hank. "They protect your legs from cactus and brush. And barbed wire. Some chaps are covered with wool. Or fur. They are good in cold weather. But they're heavy when they're wet. And they smell awful."

"Do you know what that bandanna is for, Eddie?" asked Old Ben.

"For looks, I guess," Eddie answered.

"Pulled over your mouth and nose, it keeps out the dust," said Ben.

"It can be a towel. A pot holder. A blindfold for a spooky horse. A bandage. Or a sling for a broken arm."

"I sure didn't know all that," said Eddie.

Then he asked, "Don't cowboys wear holsters and guns?"

Some of the men laughed.

"Only in the movies," said Uncle Charlie.

"Cowboys do own guns," said Old Ben. "But they don't always pack them. And they hardly ever wear a double holster. That would be very heavy."

"And uncomfortable riding all day," said Sugar Sam. "As well as dangerous."

"We kept ours in our bedrolls," said Ben. "Or in the chuck wagon when we were on a drive."

"Good," said Eddie. "Because Mom and Dad already said I couldn't have one."

Chapter 6

Old Trail Days

Sugar Sam was frying doughnuts in the cook shack. And Eddie and Old Ben were there eating them.

Some of the cowboys had gone to town. Others were off working somewhere.

"They don't know what they're missing," said Ben. He took a bite of doughnut. Then a swallow of coffee.

"Reminds me of old trail days," said Sugar Sam. "How those cowpokes could eat."

"You were a good trail cook," said Ben.

Eddie was surprised. "You mean—you mean you were on trail rides together?"

"Sure were," said Sam. "From the time we were boys. My daddy was a camp cook. I took his job after he quit."

Ben said, "Sam was a wrangler when I first met him."

"What's a 'wrangler'?" asked Eddie.

"A *wrangler* is in charge of the horses," Sam said. "It was my job to take care of the *remuda*. That's what they call the spare horses."

"There could be more than 50 horses in a remuda," said Ben. "The wrangler penned them up at night. He staked out a corral using a rope. Some horses had to be hobbled. A rope was tied from one leg to another. That kept them from running off.

"The cowboys drove the cattle. The wrangler drove the spare horses."

"That's not all the wrangler did," said Sam. "He gathered wood. Or cow chips, if there wasn't any wood. He carried water. He helped the cook."

"And he was the lowest paid," said Old Ben.

"Did you like being a cook, Sam?" asked Eddie.

"It wasn't an easy job. A cook was the first up in the morning. And the last in bed at

night." He paused. "But, yes. I liked it."

"He did more than cook," Old Ben said. "He cut hair. Sewed on buttons. And took care of us when we got sick or hurt."

"And kept the chuck wagon in order," added Sam. "It had to be packed just so. Besides food, it carried pots and pans. Bedrolls. Tools and dry firewood. Medicine and bandages. Water barrels. Stake ropes. Guns and ammunition."

"He made the best coffee too. Good and strong," said Ben. "And his vinegar pie!"

"Vinegar pie!" cried Eddie. "It sounds awful!"

Old Ben and Sugar Sam laughed. "It's better than it sounds," said Sam. "You mix water and vinegar. Add eggs, if you have some. Lots of sugar. Thicken it. Add a lump of fat. Put it between strips of dough. Then bake it."

Ben smacked his lips. Then he ate another doughnut.

Sugar Sam said, "Ben made it all the way up to trail boss."

"A trail boss gets paid more money," said Old Ben. "But he works as hard as anyone else. He's in charge of the cows and the herders."

"How many cows in a

herd?" asked Eddie.

"Over 1,000," said Ben. "Some herds were bigger. Some smaller."

"Did the cattle ever stampede?" Eddie asked.

"Many times," Old Ben answered. "That was a big danger on a drive. I've seen many men get killed in a stampede."

Sam added, "You never knew what would start a stampede. Lightning. The smell of some wild animal. The worst one I ever saw started when a cowboy sneezed."

"Most stampedes happened at night," said Ben. "There was nothing scarier than trying to head off cows in the dark."

"What was the best part of a trail drive?" Eddie asked.

Old Ben and Sugar Sam answered at the same time. "The end of it!" they said.

Chapter 7

Cowboys Then. Cowboys Now.

Eddie wanted to learn more about cowboys. So he went to the library.

He learned that cattle also came from Spain. They came with Christopher Columbus on his second voyage in 1493.

Some people thought they had been brought over even earlier by the Vikings.

The first cowboys were called *vaqueros,* a Spanish word for cow.

These early cowboys did not ride horses. They herded the cattle on foot. Some had dogs to help.

The ranchers who owned the cattle rode horses. They also owned the cowboys. The cowboys were their slaves. They did not think that a slave should ride a horse.

Herding on foot was very dangerous. The first cattle were longhorns. They often injured or killed the herders.

Over the years, the herds grew larger. Then the herders were allowed to ride horses. They became very good riders.

The vaqueros wore hats with wide brims. They were called *sombreros,* a Spanish word for *shade-maker.* They wore leather shirts and vests. And they wore long leather pants.

But they did not wear boots. Boots cost
too much. Only the rich cattle owners wore
boots.

Some wore sandals. But many went barefoot.

Surprisingly, these cowboys wore iron spurs. Even though they were barefoot.

The vaqueros were the first to rope cattle. American cowboys learned many skills from them.

Later, other breeds of cattle were brought to America. Most ranchers raised Herefords. They did better on long drives. Some drives were 2,000 miles long.

Eddie shared what he had learned. The ranch cowboys were amazed.

"A barefoot cowboy!" exclaimed Tex.

"And spurs with no boots!" cried Bud.

"A lot of things have changed," said Old Ben. "Even since I was herding. Cattle are hauled in trucks now. Ranchers drive fancy pickups. It's not the way it used to be."

"And they get paid a lot more," said Sugar Sam. "I got $20 a month when I was a wrangler. And I thought I was rich."

"I'd still like to be a cowboy," said Eddie.

"Right!" said Uncle Hank. "We better get busy. You need to learn to rope. And ride a horse."

Eddie worked hard. He did become a good rider. He learned to rope a little.

Then the big day came!

Uncle Charlie said, "Hank and I need to move some cows. We could use another hand."

"Cool!" yelled Eddie.

The horses were loaded in a trailer. Eddie climbed in the pickup. He sat between his uncles.

It was a rough drive up a steep hill. That's where the small herd was feeding.

Uncle Hank said, "They need to be moved
to fresh grass. There are only about 20 cows.
It won't take long to move them."

Eddie felt proud. He sat tall in his saddle.

They rode downhill. The cows went fast.
Uncle Hank and Uncle Charlie rode faster.

Suddenly, Eddie saw a calf trip. It rolled
down a slope. It tried to get back. But the
slope was too steep.

"Uncle Hank! Uncle Charlie!" Eddie
called.

But the cows were bawling loudly. The
men could not hear Eddie.

Eddie took the rope from the saddle horn.
His heart was pounding. He could hardly
hold the rope.

The calf bawled. Eddie saw how
frightened it was.

He twirled the rope. Around and around.
Over his head. He threw it. It fell around the
calf's neck. Eddie wrapped the rope around
the saddle horn.

"Back, Smoky!" he cried. "Back!"

Eddie pulled gently on the reins. Smoky
backed up.

The calf climbed to the top of the slope.

Uncle Charlie and Uncle Hank looked back. They watched Eddie work. They were very proud of him.

That night, Sugar Sam fixed a special meal.

"In honor of our new cowhand," he said.

All the cowboys cheered. Eddie felt very special.

Then Sam served dessert.

Eddie took a big bite. "Mmmm. Yummy! This is delicious!" he said. "What is it?"

"Vinegar pie!" laughed Sugar Sam.

"Now you're a real cowboy," said Old Ben.